Soccer Shake-Up

BY JAKE MADDOX

Text by Rebecca Wright
Illustrated by Aburtov

STONE ARCH BOOKS
a capstone imprint

Jake Maddox Sports Stories are published by Stone Arch Books
A Capstone Imprint
1710 Roe Crest Drive
North Mankato, Minnesota 56003
www.capstonepub.com

Library of Congress Cataloging-in-Publication Data
Maddox, Jake, author. Soccer shake-up / by Jake Maddox ; text by Rebecca
Wright ; illustrated by Aburtov.

    pages cm. -- (Jake Maddox Sports stories)

Summary: Worried sick about his baby brother's operation, twelve-year-old
Dominic does not really feel much like playing soccer, so he just messes
around on the field during practice — but when his grandfather teaches
him some moves he starts to take an interest and sets out to win the trust of
his coach and teammates.

ISBN 978-1-4965-0495-1 (library binding) -- ISBN 978-1-4965-0499-9 (pbk.)
-- ISBN 978-1-4965-2327-3 (ebook pdf) -- ISBN 978-1-4965-2469-0 (reflowable
epub)

1. Soccer stories. 2. Brothers--Juvenile fiction. 3. Teamwork (Sports)--
Juvenile fiction. 4. Grandfathers--Juvenile fiction. 5. Anxiety--Juvenile
fiction. [1. Soccer--Fiction. 2. Brothers--Fiction. 3. Teamwork (Sports)--
Fiction. 4. Grandfathers--Fiction. 5. Anxiety--Fiction.] I. Wright, Rebecca,
1976- author. II. Aburto, Jesus, illustrator. III. Title. IV. Series: Maddox, Jake.
Impact books. Jake Maddox sports story.

PZ7.M25643Snr 2015
813.6--dc23
[Fic]

                        2014046044

Art Director: Bob Lentz
Graphic Designer: Veronica Scott
Production Specialist: Katy LaVigne

Printed in the United States of America in Eau Claire, Wisconsin.
111915   009348R

TABLE OF CONTENTS

CHAPTER 1

WARMING THE BENCH

Twelve-year-old Dominic Harper slid into the backseat of his mom's car Monday after school. "I really don't want to play soccer," he said, crossing his arms over his chest.

"I know Caleb being sick has been hard on you," Mom said as she strapped Caleb, Dominic's two-year-old brother, into his car seat. "But you can't just stay in the house all day and play computer games."

Dominic sighed.

"This will be a much better way for you to spend your time," Mom continued. "Caleb's operation is in two weeks. After that, everything will go back to normal."

Dominic heard his mom's voice catch. Even without looking at her, he knew that there were tears in her eyes. *Might,* he thought. *She means everything* might *go back to normal.*

The problem had started months before, when Caleb suddenly became fussy all the time. Mom and Dad had been unable to figure out why he was throwing tantrums, screaming, and crying so much. He stopped sleeping through the night. Finally, the doctor had figured out what was wrong — Caleb had a tumor growing on his spine and would need surgery to remove it.

According to the doctor, the tumor was probably the harmless kind, and Caleb would likely be fine. But still, there was a small chance Caleb might have cancer, and Dominic was really worried about his brother. They wouldn't know for sure that Caleb was okay until after he had the operation.

Usually Dominic's parents limited the amount of time he spent playing computer and video games, but because they had been so worried about Caleb lately, they hadn't been enforcing the rules. Dominic had been playing video and computer games nonstop after school and on the weekends. If he couldn't sleep at night, he would get up, turn on his computer, and play some more. When he played, he didn't feel as nervous.

The past weekend, Mom had finally noticed his electronic obsession. "Dominic, you're playing too many computer games," she'd said. "Please find something else to do."

"Sure, Mom," Dominic had agreed, but he'd gone right on playing games. *It's better than sitting around worrying about Caleb,* he'd told himself.

When Mom realized Dominic hadn't stopped playing, she'd finally unplugged the computer, taken away the keyboard, and said, "That's it, Dom. I'm signing you up for soccer at the community center. It'll be good for you to get outside and run around a bit."

Without his games, the rest of the weekend had passed slowly for Dominic. Now he was off to his first soccer practice — and he was not happy about it.

When Mom stopped the car next to the soccer field, Dominic could see several boys already gathered there. A few of them were dribbling down the field doing some sort of relay race. Several other boys were sitting on the bench.

"I'm sorry I don't have time to walk you over there, Dom," Mom said. "But Caleb has an appointment soon, so I need to get going."

Dominic stayed glued to his seat and stared out the window. "I only see one kid I know," he said.

"At least you know someone!" Mom said brightly. "Now, shoo, shoo!"

"His name is Nathan," said Dominic, still firmly planted in his seat. "He's always in trouble at school."

"Oh, then maybe you should stay away from him," Mom said. "Anyway, go on! And try to have fun."

Dominic reluctantly climbed out of the car and kicked at the gravel surface of the parking lot. *This is the last thing I want to do,* he thought.

As Dominic walked over to the field, he saw Nathan and the other boys on the bench messing around and pushing each other, laughing.

A man carrying a clipboard approached Dominic. "You must be Dominic Harper. I'm Coach Everett. Welcome to the Rockets! Your mom called me earlier and said you'd be joining us today," he said. "We're doing some passing drills right now and could use another player. How about it?"

Dominic looked at the players taking turns kicking the ball on the field. "Uh, no thanks," he said.

The coach raised one eyebrow and stared at him, waiting for more explanation. Finally Dominic said, "I just don't feel like it. I think I'll just sit here on the bench for a while."

Coach Everett shook his head. "Suit yourself," he said. "But you're at soccer practice now, and I'd appreciate you joining your teammates." Then he turned away and blew his whistle to gather up the players on the field.

CHAPTER 2

TROUBLEMAKERS

Dominic didn't join his teammates — not the ones who were on the field anyway.

"Hey, Dom. What's up?" Nathan said as Dominic went to the bench and sat down.

"Not much," Dominic replied. "How come you guys aren't out on the field?"

"I'm just here because my mom thinks I need to get involved in team sports," Nathan said, rolling his eyes. "Anyway, Johnny and I were just about to have a burping contest. You want in?"

"Sounds better than playing soccer!" Dominic said. He took a deep breath and swallowed as much air as he could. A second later, he let out a loud, bold burp.

Johnny and Nathan cracked up and tried to match Dominic's burp. The three boys kept going, each one trying to outdo the others, until the rest of the team finally came over to the bench for a water break.

As the rest of the team lined up at the watercooler, one player marched over to Dominic, Johnny, and Nathan, looking irritated. "If you're not going to play, could you at least stop being so distracting?" he snapped. "We've got a big game coming up, and these drills will help with our offense."

"But, Seth . . . we're the cheerleaders," Johnny replied. "Cheerleaders are supposed to be loud!"

"Why didn't you just stay home?" Seth asked. "You're already bringing the team down, and it's only the first practice."

Nathan stood up, looking like he was about to argue back. Before he could, Coach walked over and interrupted.

"Enough!" he said. "Everyone out on the field!" He looked sternly at Dominic, Johnny, and Nathan. "That means you three as well."

The boys obeyed, but the fun continued on the field. Dominic, Johnny, and Nathan laughed and pushed each other while they waited in line for their turns, ignoring the glares coming at them from their teammates.

During one drill, when Dom was supposed to be passing to a teammate, he purposely kicked the ball in the wrong direction. Nathan and Johnny cracked up in response.

By then, Coach had had enough. "All right, you three. Back to the bench!" he shouted.

Dominic walked over to the bench and lay on his back so he could stare up at the clouds. *I can't believe I have to be here every day. Soccer practice is so boring,* he thought. *I'd much rather be at the doctor's office with Mom and Caleb. At least then I would know what's going on with him.*

At the thought of his brother, Dominic's stomach ached in a familiar, anxious way. It always did that when he thought about Caleb and what might happen to him because of his illness.

He'll be okay, Dominic told himself. *He has to be.*

When practice was finally over, Seth marched over to the bench, where Dominic was still reclining.

"Why did you even join the team?" Seth demanded. "Some of us actually take soccer seriously."

"None of your business," Dominic snapped. He turned away, grabbed his things, and started walking toward the parking lot to look for his mom.

It's none of your business that I don't actually want to be here. It's no one's business that my brother might be really sick and that the only thing that distracts me from worrying is playing computer games, Dominic thought. *It's no one's business but my own.*

CHAPTER 3

CARLOS'S MOVES

When Dominic arrived at practice Tuesday afternoon, he felt sick to his stomach. Caleb had been extra fussy on the car ride over to the field, and his body had started shaking as if he was cold, even though it was seventy degrees outside.

Dominic's mom had been so concerned that she'd called Caleb's doctor. The doctor had assured them it was probably just a reaction to Caleb's new medication, but Dominic was still worried.

He wanted to go home, but Mom had insisted it would be good for him to be active — that it would take his mind off things.

Dominic reluctantly made his way over to the bench. Johnny and Nathan were already there. A moment later, Coach Everett approached the three of them.

"Look, guys. I need you out on the field, and I really need you to work hard today," Coach said. "Our first game is a week from Saturday, and we're up against our league rival — the Warriors. Carlos won't be here for the game, and we'll need all the help we can get. This is our last practice until next week, so we need to make the most of it."

"Who's Carlos?" Dominic asked, looking around at the other players.

"I am," said a boy wearing a red jersey. He was standing by the watercooler filling up his water bottle. "If you had played with the team for more than five minutes yesterday, you might remember me."

"Wait," Dominic said. "How come we're not practicing again until next week?"

Coach gave him a frustrated look. "If you had been paying attention yesterday, you'd know that the community center is getting some work done on the field at the end of the week," he said. "Practice is canceled until Monday, so today's practice is extra important. Let's get going. We've already broken into two teams to scrimmage."

Johnny and Nathan stood up to join the team on the field, but Dominic stayed seated. "I'll just watch," he said.

"Have it your way, Dominic," Coach replied. "I can't force you to play. But if you're going to sit on the bench, I at least want you watching and encouraging your teammates." He turned around and walked out to center field.

Dominic crossed his arms and watched from the bench. He stared out at the field just in time to see Carlos score a goal.

"Way to go, Carlos!" the players shouted.

The two teams met at the center circle again for the kickoff. Right away, Carlos got control of the ball and dribbled down the field. Another player tried to steal the ball, but Carlos faked him out, doing a quick half-turn in the other direction and dribbling toward the goal.

Wow, Dominic thought. *Carlos is good.*

Dominic was watching the field so closely that he didn't even notice Coach Everett had sat down beside him.

"Hey, Dominic," the coach said. "I wanted to talk to you. I heard your little brother is sick."

"He'll probably be fine," Dominic said, looking down at his feet. "We'll find out next week, after his operation."

Coach nodded. "Still, it must be hard on your whole family," he said.

Dominic shrugged and looked at the ground. He didn't want to talk about this. Not here. Not with his coach.

"Come on out and practice. It might help get your mind off things," Coach said, smiling slightly. "I'd like to see you kick the ball at least once today."

"Fine," Dominic said reluctantly. He stood up slowly and walked toward the field, but when play began, he avoided the ball. Instead, he jogged up and down the field, pretending like he was trying to get open. But Dominic also watched Carlos — his fakes, his cuts toward the goal, his crisp passes.

It is nice to get moving, Dominic admitted to himself. *But if I can't play like Carlos, what's the point of playing at all?*

CHAPTER 4

FAKE-OUT

As the week continued, so did Caleb's fussiness. After bringing him to the doctor, Mom and Dad had decided he should stay in the hospital until his surgery the following week. That meant Dominic was spending much of his free time at his grandpa's house.

On Friday afternoon, after Dominic had spent the past two afternoons watching TV in the living room, Grandpa came in from doing yard work and sat down beside him.

"Hey," Grandpa said. "How 'bout helping me do some raking before it gets dark?"

Ugh, Dominic thought. *I can't really say no to Grandpa.* Instead, he forced a smile and said, "Sure. I'll meet you out there."

* * *

Dominic trudged into the garage and picked out a rake. As he walked into the backyard, Grandpa called, "Look what I found!"

Before Dominic could reply, Grandpa kicked a soccer ball to him. The ball sailed right to Dominic's feet.

"Grandpa," Dominic said, surprised, "that was a good kick!"

"I played a little soccer in my day," Grandpa said.

"I didn't know that," Dominic said. "Want to teach me some moves? My team has our first game in a week."

"You bet I do!" Grandpa said, smiling. "Show me your dribbling."

Dominic dribbled across the yard, but the ball kept getting out too far in front of him. When he managed to keep it closer to his feet, he almost tripped over it.

"Instead of kicking the ball so far ahead, try giving it some light taps," Grandpa said. "It makes it harder for a defender to steal it. Kick the ball over, and I'll show you."

Dominic kicked the ball to his grandpa, who trapped the ball and dribbled across the yard, tapping the ball between his feet.

When he reached the edge of the yard, Grandpa ran at the ball like he was about to give it a hard kick. Instead, he put his foot on top of it, rolled it backward, and dribbled in the opposite direction.

"First, you have to get good at handling the ball," Grandpa called, still dribbling. "The point of a fake, like the one I just did, is to help you break away from a defender."

Grandpa paused, thinking for a minute. Then he said, "Wait here. I'll show you the best way to practice dribbling."

When Grandpa came back a couple minutes later, he was carrying a tennis ball. "Dribbling a tennis ball is like running with weights on your ankles," he said. "When you take the weights off, you run faster. After you get used to dribbling a tennis ball, dribbling a soccer ball will feel easy."

Dominic tried dribbling the tennis ball and tripped over his feet. He laughed. It was difficult, but he was having fun. And for once, he wasn't worrying about Caleb.

After Dominic did one particularly good fake, Grandpa whistled. "Look at you! You're getting good!" he shouted.

"Maybe someday I'll get as good as Carlos," Dominic said.

"Who's Carlos?" asked Grandpa.

"A kid on my team," Dom said. "I've never seen anyone play like he does before."

"Have you ever seen a professional soccer game?" Grandpa asked.

Dominic shook his head.

Grandpa glanced at his watch. "Well, you're in luck," he said. "I think there's a game on now. Come on."

The two of them headed inside to watch the game, grabbing snacks on the way. As they settled onto the couch and turned on the TV, Dominic was impressed right away.

"These players are amazing. Even better than Carlos!" Dominic said as he watched the players passing, dodging, faking, and dribbling. "This is awesome!"

"Yes, it is," Grandpa agreed, smiling.

CHAPTER 5

UPS AND DOWNS

Dominic spent the rest of the weekend at Grandpa's house. Even though Caleb's operation wasn't until Friday, their parents were staying at a hotel near the hospital so they could check on Caleb every day.

Sunday morning, Dominic's mom called to say he'd be staying at his Grandpa's for the rest of the week, too. Mom picked him up so he could get more clothes from home, then dropped him back off at Grandpa's with a promise to call and check in each night.

Dominic felt nervous for his brother, and he hated not knowing what was going on. Since there were no video or computer games at Grandpa's, Dom turned to soccer. He and Grandpa spent a few hours practicing outside on Sunday afternoon, and that evening, they watched an exciting professional soccer game on TV. After a full day of soccer, Dominic finally started to feel calm again.

* * *

On Monday afternoon, Dominic arrived at the soccer field for practice. For the first time, he was excited to play with the team. He and Grandpa arrived early, before anyone else. They brought a soccer ball with them so Dom could get some extra practice in before the rest of the team arrived.

Dominic kicked the ball out to the field and chased after it while Grandpa watched. "Let's see you dribble, kid!" he called.

Dominic took the ball down the field and back, touching the ball lightly with the insides of his feet like Grandpa had taught him. He was so focused on his dribbling that he didn't even notice someone else was there.

Suddenly, Coach shouted from the sidelines: "Dominic, you're a natural! Great ball control. Remember to look up when you can, so you can avoid defenders."

Dom glanced up and grinned. Coach Everett was standing beside Grandpa, and both were watching him.

"Sure thing, Coach!" Dominic called back.

The rest of the players began arriving, and the team started warming up. After a few minutes of passing back and forth in partners, the Rockets lined up for drills.

They worked on passing, defense, and corner kicks. Dom's teammates — with the exception of Nathan and Johnny, who sat on the sideline — seemed excited that he had decided to take the field. They cheered him on in drills and sprints.

After practice, Carlos came up to Dom and gave him a high five. "Hey, you looked good out there today," he said. "Can't wait to see what you'll do in an actual game."

"Thanks, Carlos," Dominic said, smiling. Practice had been tough, but it had left him feeling invigorated. When he was playing, that anxious aching in his stomach disappeared, and he had *fun*.

* * *

That Friday, the day of Caleb's surgery, Dominic was feeling more anxious than ever. He showed up to practice because Grandpa had forced him to, but Dominic did not want to be there.

I should be at home waiting for Mom's call to hear how the operation went, he thought.

Coach called a huddle at the beginning of practice, but Dominic spaced out and didn't listen. When the team took the field, Dominic went to sit on sideline with Nathan and Johnny, who were fooling around as usual. Their jokes and pranks were the perfect distraction.

When the rest of the team was scrimmaging, Nathan and Johnny dared Dominic to skip back and forth along the sideline, singing "Mary Had a Little Lamb."

Dominic took the dare, singing, "Her fleece was white as snoooooooow!" and skipping as high in the air as he could. The rest of the players paused, confused by the scene.

"Keep playing, team!" Coach called. "Don't pay attention to the distraction." Then, to Dominic, he said, "If you can't take this seriously, Dominic, you'll have to sit out of the game tomorrow night."

Embarrassed that Coach had yelled at him in front of everyone, Dominic shouted back, "I don't even want to play! In fact, I hope we lose tomorrow!" He stomped over to gather his things, not saying a word to Nathan or Johnny. Then he went to sit at a picnic table by the parking lot, where he waited until Grandpa came to get him.

CHAPTER 6

RESULTS

After practice, Dominic got into the car without saying goodbye to anyone — even ignoring Johnny and Nathan.

Grandpa could tell something was wrong right away. "How was practice today?" he asked.

"I don't want to talk about it," Dominic replied. "I just want to know how Caleb's doing."

"We haven't heard anything yet, but they should be calling any minute," Grandpa said. "There's a soccer game on tonight. What do you say we watch it while we wait?"

Dominic smiled. At least it would be a distraction. "Sure thing, Grandpa," he replied.

As soon as they got home, Dominic and Grandpa grabbed a snack from the kitchen, but before they could do anything else, Grandpa's phone rang. Immediately, Dominic felt his stomach get tight with worry.

"Hello?" Grandpa said into the phone. Then he paused for a minute.

Dominic stood still as he watched, almost afraid to move.

"Oh, thank goodness!" Grandpa cried. He wiped tears from his eyes, but Dominic could tell they were happy tears.

"Was that Mom?" Dominic asked when Grandpa had hung up. "What'd she say?"

"They won't know for sure until the lab results are back tomorrow, but the doctors removed the growth, and they think the tumor is the harmless kind," Grandpa replied. "If the results are good, they'll all come home tomorrow."

Dominic hugged his grandpa. For the first time in months, he felt truly happy.

* * *

When Dominic woke up the next morning, he was relieved thinking about Caleb's surgery. But then he remembered something else — his soccer game tonight.

I really messed up at practice yesterday, he thought. *I have to make it up to my teammates by putting in my best effort in the game tonight.*

Dom spent the day practicing his moves outside and watching soccer games on TV.

When it was nearly time to go, Grandpa stuck his head out the back door and called to Dom, "You almost ready, champ?"

Dominic ran inside, filled up his water bottle, gathered his soccer equipment, and headed to the car.

* * *

When Dominic arrived at the field, the sun was starting to set, and the floodlights over the field had been turned on. Most of his teammates were already warming up. Dom went onto the field to join them, but no one said hi or even looked in his direction.

They must be upset about yesterday. Can't really blame them, Dominic thought, so he went to sit on the bench instead.

Soon Coach walked over and sat down. "Hey, Dominic. Can we talk about what happened yesterday?" he said. "I'm upset that you weren't taking practice seriously, and I think some of your teammates are upset, too."

Dominic sighed. "I wasn't being a good teammate, and I'm sorry for yelling at you," he said. "I was having a bad day. My brother had his surgery yesterday, and we'll find out today if he's okay or not."

"That must be scary. But the way you were acting yesterday wasn't acceptable, even if you were nervous about your brother. In the future, I'd rather you come talk to me than disrupt practice," Coach said.

Dominic nodded in response.

"In the meantime," Coach continued, "I think some soccer will do you good. It'll give you something else to focus on — like having a good game." With that, Coach smiled, stood up, and walked out to center field for the coin toss.

The Rockets won the toss and chose to kick off. The referee placed the ball at the center of the field and stepped back. Dylan, the Rockets' center forward, ran up and passed the ball to his teammate on the left, David. They tried to advance, but one of the Warriors darted in, stole the ball, and broke toward his team's goal.

The Warriors' player passed the ball to a teammate, who gave it a strong kick into the net. After just forty-five seconds of play, the Warriors had scored their first goal.

The ball was put back into play, and two of the Rockets passed the ball back and forth as they moved up the field. But when they got inside the goalie box, a Warriors' defender lunged and stole the ball away, knocking it out of the defensive zone.

The Warriors managed to advance the ball all the way to the Rockets' defensive zone before Nathan attempted to steal it. He darted forward, but since he hadn't practiced much, he ended up tripping the player with the ball.

"Foul!" shouted the referee, pointing at Nathan. "Penalty kick for the Warriors!"

The Rockets groaned as they got positioned on defense for the penalty kick. The Warriors player ran at the ball and kicked it hard into the right-hand corner of the net. The score was now 0–2.

CHAPTER 7

TIME-OUT

At halftime, the Rockets were still down by two. The players were all sitting on the bench when Dom glanced up and saw his parents walking over from the parking lot.

Dominic was shocked. *What are they doing here?* he wondered.

His first thought was that something had gone wrong with Caleb. But then he saw that his mother was carrying Caleb, who was asleep on her shoulder, and he could tell how relieved they all were. Dominic ran over to them, eager to see his little brother.

"The doctor said Caleb is going to be fine," Mom said, handing Caleb to Dad and giving Dominic a tight hug.

Dominic's stomach did flips. "Hey, buddy!" he said to his little brother, pulling gently on his foot. "You excited to see me play some soccer?" Caleb responded with a sleepy smile.

"How's the game going?" Dad asked.

"Not good," Dominic said. "The score is 0–2."

"Well, there's still time," said Grandpa. "Let's see what you can do out there."

As his family went to sit by the other fans, Dominic joined his teammates, who were gathered around Coach in a huddle.

Dom tapped his coach on the shoulder. "Coach," he said, "can I go in soon?"

Coach nodded. "Can you promise me you'll focus on the game?"

Dominic nodded eagerly. "You got it, Coach."

"Okay, how about you take Dylan's place at center forward," Coach said. "On the next break in play, you can go in."

Dominic was nervous and excited as he got ready to sub in for Dylan. He could hear Johnny and Nathan sitting on the bench and making gross noises by blowing into the crooks of their elbows. The noise was so distracting that Coach called a time-out after a couple minutes and pulled Dominic aside.

"Dom, I really need your help," Coach said. "Your friends are distracting the team. I've tried everything. Could you talk to them before you go in?"

"I'll try," Dominic said.

As the ball was put in play again, Dominic went over to Nathan and Johnny. "Come on, guys," he said. "My parents are here, and I really want to play. Can you knock it off for a while?"

"Nah, I don't feel like it," Nathan said. He and Johnny both laughed.

"You guys," Dominic said, "the team is in trouble, but I think we can help! Maybe it will be fun."

"Fun would be if my parents stopped making me come here," Nathan said.

"Look," Dominic said, "My family is here and I —"

"Okay, okay. Just leave us alone," Johnny said. "We'll be quiet."

As Dominic turned back toward the field, he heard the spectators cheer. The Rockets had scored their first goal. The score was 1–2.

Dominic ran over to Coach Everett. "They promised to stay quiet," he said. "Can I go in please?"

Coach smiled. "All right," he said. "You're in. Tell Dylan to take a breather."

Dominic ran onto the field as quickly as he could.

CHAPTER 8

TAKING THE FIELD

Dominic watched his teammates pass the ball back and forth, but even when he was wide open, he never got the ball. He was frustrated, but after skipping out on practice yesterday, Dom understood why they wouldn't pass to him. They thought he was a goof-off.

Next time he was open, Dominic waved his arms and shouted, "Over here!"

But Seth had the ball. He looked right at Dominic, then passed to another teammate.

I have to do something to prove myself, Dominic thought. *But what?*

Just then, a nearby Warriors' player stole the ball from the one of the Rockets. Dominic saw his opening. Nobody — not even the players on the other team — were paying much attention to him.

I'll use that to my advantage, he thought. *No one will see me coming.*

Dominic darted forward and stole the ball back from the opposing player. Almost immediately, three Warriors swarmed him.

Finally, Dominic thought. He pretended he was about to dribble to the goal, but just when the other players near him started to run forward, he put his foot on top of the ball, pulled it back toward him, spun around, and headed in a different direction.

Dominic had a head start toward the goal, but soon two Warriors were beside him again. Dominic did another fake, pretending to go toward the sideline, but then he turned and darted forward with the ball. The other players were left in his dust. Now there was nobody between him and the other team's goal.

Dominic was only ten feet from the goal, but the goalie was waiting for him, ready to keep him from scoring. Remembering the fakes Grandpa had taught him, Dom pretended he was about to kick the ball directly into the net. But at the last minute, he spun and kicked as hard as he could into the far upper corner of the net.

Dominic watched as the ball hit the net, hardly able to believe he'd just tied the game.

CHAPTER 9

FINAL MINUTES

After Dominic's goal, the Warriors took possession of the ball at the centerline. A few minutes later, though, one of the Rockets' players stole it. Just like before, the Rockets kept passing the ball back and forth, but they were having trouble advancing down the field and toward the opposing team's goal.

The Rockets still weren't passing to Dominic. Only this time, there was a different reason.

The Warriors are guarding me too closely, Dominic thought. *Every time I move, at least two defenders follow me.*

Johnny, however, was also on the field and was standing wide open near the sideline. With his reputation as a troublemaker, none of the Rockets were even thinking about passing to him. He was in the exact position Dominic had been in just a short time ago.

"Two minutes left!" Coach Everett shouted.

Dominic desperately tried to get free so someone could pass the ball to him. At last, he saw his chance. One of the Warriors guarding him got distracted, and Dominic darted forward, away from the other defender.

Sure enough, one of Dominic's teammates spotted him and passed him the ball. Once he had the ball, Dominic took off. Three Warriors defenders stood between him and the goal, but he faked each of them out until he was alone and inside the 18-yard box.

But the goalie was ready. He stood with his arms out, expecting Dominic to pull another fake and shoot in the opposite direction.

Just then, Johnny ran down the sideline toward the other side of the goal, about ten feet from Dominic. The goalie, who was still focused on Dominic, didn't seem to notice him.

There couldn't be more than a minute left in the game. Dominic knew he had to do something — and quick.

He drew back his leg, pretending he was about to kick the ball as hard as he could into the goal, but at the last minute, he spun around and passed it to Johnny, who was waiting on the opposite side of the goal.

Johnny seemed slightly surprised and fumbled the ball, but he recovered quickly. The goalie didn't have time to get to the other side, so Johnny easily kicked the ball into the goal.

There was whooping and cheering from the sidelines as the Rockets took the lead 3–2.

Dominic looked over at his family. They were cheering and clapping. Caleb, awake now and sitting in his mother's lap, also clapped his hands.

There were only thirty seconds left in the game — not enough time for anything more to happen. The Warriors passed the ball back and forth a few times, but soon the referee blew his whistle.

The game was over.

The Rockets gathered to celebrate, high-fiving each other and then lining up to shake hands with the Warriors.

As everyone gathered up their things, Coach said, "Don't forget practice on Monday. Our second game is next Saturday night, and we need to keep working hard!"

Dominic grabbed his bag and hurried over to his family. He couldn't wait to give his little brother a hug.

Forget practice? Dominic thought as he left the field. *I can hardly wait!*

AUTHOR BIO

Rebecca Wright writes short stories and novels for young readers. In her free time, she enjoys playing and watching soccer, reading, and cooking.

ILLUSTRATOR BIO

Aburtov has worked as a colorist for Marvel, DC, IDW, and Dark Horse and as an illustrator for Stone Arch Books. He lives in Monterrey, Mexico, with his lovely wife, Alba, and his crazy children, Ilka, Mila, and Aleph.

GLOSSARY

ache (AKE) — to hurt in a way that is constant but not severe

anxious (ANGK-shuhss) — worried

embarrassed (em-BARE-uhsst) — made someone feel ashamed and uncomfortable

focused (FOH-kuhsst) — concentrated

fumbled (FUHM-buhld) — in sports: lost control of the ball after you have touched it

impressed (im-PRESST) — made people think highly of you

professional (pruh-FESH-uh-nuhl) — in sports: making money for doing something others do for fun

reaction (ree-AK-shuhn) — an action in response to something

reluctantly (ri-LUHK-tuhnt-lee) — done with hesitation

reputation (REP-yuh-TAY-shuhn) — your character as judged by other people

scrimmage (SKRIM-ij) — an informal game, often done for practice

surgery (SUR-jur-ee) — medical treatment that involves repairing, removing, or replacing injured or diseased parts of the body

tumor (TOO-mur) — an abnormal mass of cells in the body

DISCUSSION QUESTIONS

1. Dominic discovers that soccer is a good activity for him to do when he is feeling nervous about his brother's health. Do you have a hobby that always makes you feel better? Talk about it.

2. When Dominic gets really nervous, he ends up fooling around instead of playing as part of the team. What do you think he could've done differently in these situations? Talk about the possibilities.

3. Even though Dominic struggles with soccer at first, he practices and improves so that he can help his team. Discuss a time when you had to practice in order to get better at something.

WRITING PROMPTS

1. Imagine you are a member of Dominic's family. Write a paragraph about how you would deal with Caleb's illness.

2. Grandpa helps Dominic improve at soccer and is there for him when he's upset. Pretend you are Grandpa, and write a letter to Dominic showing your support.

3. How would the ending of this book be different if the Rockets had lost to the Warriors? Write a different final chapter to this story.

SOCCER DICTIONARY

- **18-yard box** — the area near each goal that extends 18 yards to each side of the goal; also known as the "penalty area"

- **assist** — a pass or other action that helps a teammate score

- **corner kick** — a free kick from a corner of the field near an opposing team's goal

- **defenders** — players who are situated near their team's goal and contribute primarily to defense

- **fake** — a quick movement, such as pretending to kick, pass, or dribble, designed to trick an opponent

- **forwards** — players who play near the opponent's goal, focusing on offense

- **foul** — an action that is against the rules

- **goal kick** — a free kick that is given to a defensive player when an opposing player drives the ball out of bounds over the end line

- **header** — a shot or pass made by hitting the soccer ball with your head

- **kickoff** — the kick that starts play in a soccer game

- **midfielders** — players that normally play toward the middle of the field, contributing equally to offense and defense

- **offside** — in a position on the opponent's side of the field where a player isn't supposed to be during a game

- **penalty kick** — a free kick at the goal, granted because of fouls or other violations that occur near the goal

- **throw-in** — a throw made from a player on the sideline to put the ball back in play

- **trap** — to stop and gain control of the soccer ball without using your hands

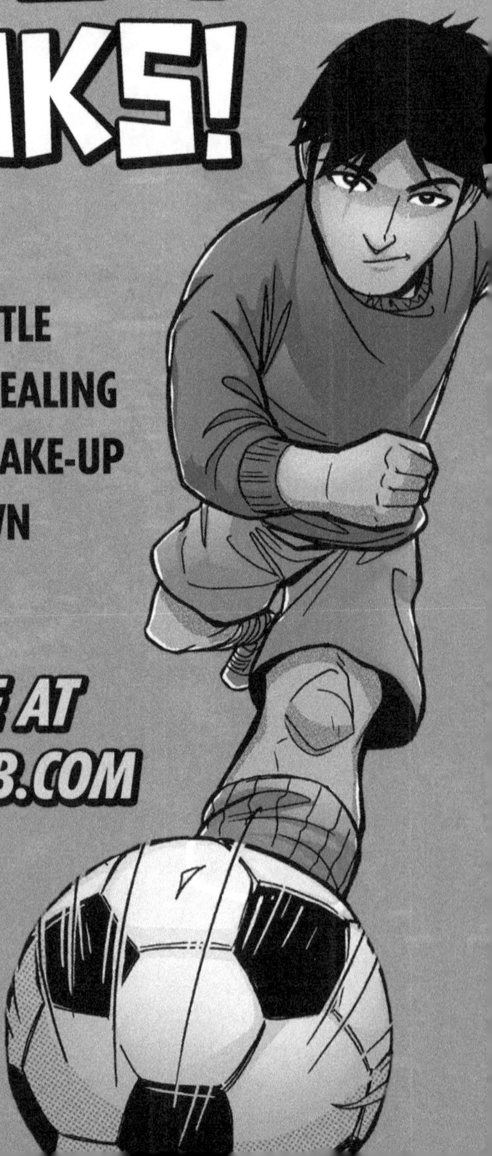

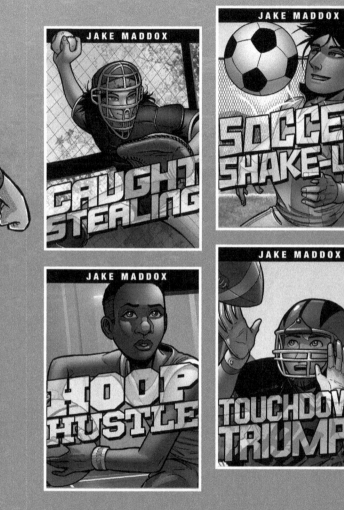

READ THEM ALL !